Philomena wonderpen

is a very naughty teacher

Hi, I'm Philomena Wonderpen. My best friend, George, sometimes calls me Philomena Daydreamer. I looove daydreams.

Imagine if you could draw your dreams with a magic pen.

What would you draw? A beautiful black horse? A magic carpet? Or even better, would you make yourself the teacher? Then you could boss the whole class!

If only daydreams could come true...

Published by
Happy Cat Books
An imprint of Catnip Publishing Ltd
14 Greville Street
London EC1N 8SB

First published by Penguin Books, Australia, 2006

This edition first published 2008
1 3 5 7 9 10 8 6 4 2

A CIP catalogue record for this book is available from the British Library

ISBN 978-1-905117-75-8

Printed in Poland

www.catnippublishing.co.uk

Philomena
wonderpen
is a very naughty teacher

HAPPY CAT BOOKS

ian bone   illustrated by janine dawson

chapter 1

Philomena Wonderpen knew that
something big was about to happen.
She could feel it. She could smell it.
She could even taste it.

Or was that the cloud biscuits from her
dream she was tasting?

Then she remembered what the

big thing was, and

jumped

out of bed.

She s t r e t c h e d herself in front of her mirror, but her fingers *still* couldn't touch the ceiling. She wriggled her legs. They were the same bothersome size as yesterday.

'Trust George Creek to get it wrong,' she sighed. George was her un-best friend. He'd told her she'd wake up bigger on her eighth birthday. 'And that's today!'

George had told her this amazing fact last week while he was eating a biscuit. 'I know all about being eight,' he said, which was funny because he was only seven. 'You'll wake up HUGE!

It happened to my cousin Bethany. Honest. She was just a little titch, then along comes her eighth birthday and wham!'

George had shot biscuit crumbs into the air when he said 'Wham!'

Philomena stood up to watch them fly. They looked like a thousand little cousin Bethanys spinning to the moon. Maybe one of them would give her a ride. Then they'd get to eat moon-cake for breakfast and lunch and dinner . . .

'Philomena!'

That was George, breaking a perfectly fine daydream.

'What?' said Philomena.

George leaned closer. 'You're not really a year older on your birthday, you know,' he said. 'You're only one day older than yesterday. And that's a fact, Philomena Wonderpen.'

George always said, 'And that's a fact'.

Philomena sighed. 'I don't want to be only *one* day older.'

Which was when George had said that Philomena was his un-best friend, because she simply couldn't accept a good fact.

Philomena wasn't worried. They'd been un-best friends before. She knew George would change his mind. He'd even be happy that she wasn't HUGE. Or living on the moon.

Back in her bedroom, Philomena twirled herself around in front of the mirror. Her fingers started tingling. Was that normal for an eight-year-old? They'd never tingled when she was seven. Maybe they were trying to tell her something?

Then Philomena realised:

'It's present time!'

She dressed herself quickly and ran to the door.

chapter 2

As Philomena skipped down the hallway, she passed
a picture on the wall. It was a portrait of Great
Grandfather Rufus Wonderpen.

'Good morning,
Great Grandfather,' called Philomena.

Then she stopped. There was something different
about the picture this morning. Was Great Grandfather's
pen glimmering? Philomena went back to the picture.
Great Grandfather Rufus was holding the very first
wonder pen ever made. He'd designed it himself. These
days, wonder pens were made in factories and sold
all over the world. Philomena put her nose up to the
picture. The wonder pen looked the same as always.

Philomena straightened Great Grandfather Rufus's
picture frame. 'Done a good drawing lately?' she asked.

The Wonderpens always asked each other this
question. Great Grandfather Rufus didn't reply.
He was only a picture, after all.

Philomena skipped to the kitchen. She wondered how many presents would be waiting for her. An enormous mountain of coloured boxes? A pile so high it would burst through the ceiling?

'Happy birthday, darling,' said her parents, when she entered the kitchen.

Philomena looked around. There didn't seem to be a **gigantic** **pile** anywhere. There were no coloured boxes lurking in the corners, either. In fact, she couldn't see any presents at all. Then she noticed her dad was hiding something behind his back.

'Well, well,' he said. 'Eight.'

'I am,' said Philomena.

Dad drew the number eight in the air with his finger. Philomena laughed. Her dad was the big boss at the wonder pen factory, and here he was drawing numbers in the air.

Mum nudged him. 'The present,' she whispered.

Dad pulled a small present out from behind his back and handed it to Philomena.

'Happy Birthday,'

said her parents.

'Thank you sooo much,' said Philomena.

She removed the ribbon and wrapping paper from the present. Now she had a long, velvet box in her hand. It looked like the kind they sold wonder pens in. She opened the lid. There was a pen inside. It looked a lot like a wonder pen. In fact, it *was* a wonder pen.

'That's your very own wonder pen,' said Dad.

'Isn't it wonderful?' said Mum.

Philomena tried very hard to smile. She tried even harder to look like she was happy to get a wonder pen for her birthday. But . . . well . . .

Philomena sighed a tiny sigh.

There were wonder pens *all* over her house. She could see two on the kitchen bench. And another was lying on the floor where someone had dropped it. And there were three in her dad's top pocket.

'I suppose I've never had my own wonder pen before,' said Philomena.

Dad winked at her. Then he put on a serious, factory-boss kind of look. 'Phillie,' he said. 'Now that you're eight, there's something you should know . . .'

'I already know,' said Philomena. 'I'm not any bigger, if that's what you mean.'

Dad smiled and shook his head. He was about to say something else, when Philomena's little brother, Tobias, walked into the room.

'I'm hungry!' he whined.

Dad leaned over towards Philomena. 'Later,' he whispered, 'I'll tell you *all* about the Wonderpens.' Then he started cracking eggs for breakfast.

Philomena sat down at the table. She wondered what her dad meant. Was he going to tell her about the wonder pens he made in the factory? Or about her family, the Wonderpens?

She twirled her birthday present in her hands. It caught little snaps of sunlight as it spun. For just a moment her pen looked like a twinkling star.

Philomena stopped **twirling** her pen and looked at it closely. The snaps were gone.

Mum sat down and smiled at Philomena. 'Done a good drawing lately?' she asked.

Philomena shrugged. 'Not lately.'

'Why don't you draw one now, with your pen?'

'*I* want to draw,' said Tobias, reaching for the wonder pen.

'Oh, no you don't,' said Dad.

Mum picked Tobias up and whizzed him around the room.

Dad squatted next to Philomena. 'Imagine if you could choose the coolest, most amazing way to get to school today,' he said. 'What would it be?'

Philomena grinned. That wasn't fair. He knew she'd imagine a thousand ways to get to school.

'Just the one?' she said.

Dad nodded. He loved playing games like this.

Philomena forgot about birthday presents and closed her eyes. She saw a swirl of pictures in her head. There were so many cool ways to get to school. She could travel on a camel train, ten thousand camels long. Or

float along on a *magic* carpet.

Or maybe . . . ? Yes.

'I would ride to school on a beautiful, black horse,' she said. 'And I'd call him Black Thunder, and he would run like the wind.'

Her mum smiled. 'You could draw the horse with your new pen,' she said.

'Do a drawing, do a drawing!' yelled Tobias.

Philomena's fingers started tingling again. She grabbed a piece of paper and started to draw. Her wonder pen flew across the page. She made Black Thunder tall. He had a shiny, dark coat with white socks and a white diamond on his nose. It *would* be wonderful to ride him to school. She'd lean forward in the saddle and whisper in his ear, 'Run like the wind, Black Thunder.' And oh, how he would run.

Philomena sighed, then she muttered under her breath, 'I wish . . .'

Her pen suddenly felt warm in her hand. For just a moment, Philomena thought she saw twirling lines reflected in the metal. But when she looked closer, they were gone.

'Just another dream,' she sighed.

Her nickname at school was Philomena Daydreamer. Even her teacher, Mr Flower, was always telling her to take her head out of the clouds.

Just then a car horn **beeped** outside. Mrs Creek and George had come to drive her.

'Oh my gosh,' said Philomena. 'I'll be late for school!'

'Philomena, there's something I haven't told you,' said Dad urgently.

'Haven't got time, Dad,' said Philomena, looking around for her school bag.

'But you really should know,' he said.

'Later,' she said, putting the wonder pen away in its box. Then she slipped it into her bag.

The car horn **beeped** again.

'Bye Mum, Dad, Tobes!' Philomena ran out the door.

'But . . . your horse!' called Dad.

'Put it on the fridge,' said Philomena as she climbed into the car.

chapter 3

Mrs Creek started singing **'Happy Birthday'**
as soon as the car door was closed. Even George
joined in. They sang so loudly that Philomena
couldn't hear what her parents were trying to tell
her outside the car. They were yelling and pointing
at something.

Then Mrs Creek started driving away. Philomena
turned to wave goodbye, and just caught sight of
a black, flicking horse tail vanishing round
the corner of her house.

'Could that be . . . ?' whispered Philomena.

'Could that be what?' said George.

'I saw something,' said Philomena.

'You're always seeing something,' said George.

Philomena sat back in the seat and clutched her bag
to herself. George was right. She *was* always wishing
for things that really should not be there. 'Even so,'
she said, 'I'd love to have Black Thunder.'

'What?' said George, looking at the sky. 'Thunder? It doesn't look like it will rain.'

'No. My horse . . .' began Philomena.

'Did you get a horse for your birthday?'

'No. I got a pen.'

Now George was confused. Philomena knew how he felt. Had she really seen a black, flicking horse tail? Or had she imagined it? Maybe that was what Dad had been trying to tell her in the kitchen. That she got more than just a silly old wonder pen for her birthday. That they had given her a horse!

'You look smaller, not bigger,' said George.

'That's because I didn't go **WHAM!**

on my birthday,' Philomena said.

'And I didn't go **BAM!**

or **SLAM!**

either.'

George smiled. 'And that's a fact,' he said.

Then they both started laughing. Trust George to
make her happy again. She wanted to ask him if he'd
seen a black horse at her house, but he was too busy
talking about their teacher.

'Mr Flower will let you sit in the birthday chair
today,' he said.

Another fact. Sitting in the birthday chair meant
you got to do very sensible things, like run the class
meeting. Philomena tried to remember how to run a
class meeting. There were rules, but she couldn't think
what they were. Her fingers started tingling again.

How could she run
a meeting with tingling
fingers?

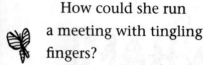

Maybe they would stop
if she listened very hard to
George. He liked talking almost as much
as he liked facts. Philomena concentrated, but her
fingers started crawling towards the wonder pen in
her bag. She grabbed them and whispered, 'Stop that!'
They didn't want to stop. They crept like thieves. She
put them under her arms and they tickled her. She sat
on them and they pinched her bottom! So she set
them free. They removed the wonder pen, took
out her lunch-order bag and started drawing.

'Something quick,' whispered Philomena.

Butterflies.

She drew one, two, five, ten butterflies.
She drew stripy butterflies and spotted butterflies.

When she was finished she thought, 'What would
happen if they came to life and tickled George's nose?'
The thought made her smile.

'I wish . . .' she sighed.

Suddenly George cried out, 'Hey! Stop that!'

'Stop what?' said Philomena.

George wound down his window and Philomena

saw one, two, five, ten pairs of little wings fly out of the car.

'What were they?' she asked.

'Moths,' said George, knowingly. 'Tiger moths, probably. Or leopard moths . . .'

Philomena wanted to ask George if he was sure, but she didn't. George was *always* sure. She looked out the window for the little wings. They were all gone.

Mrs Creek pulled up at the school gates, and Philomena and George *tumbled* out of the car.

As they entered the playground, Philomena thought she saw something flutter past her eyes.

'You know, George,' she said. 'I think today is going to be a *very* wonderful, *very* big day.'

George looked at her and grinned. 'Of course it is,' he said. 'And that's a fact!'

chapter 4

George ran around the schoolyard telling everyone it was Philomena's birthday. Then they met up with Philomena's other best friends, Angie Christouphous and Minna Lim.

'What did you get for your birthday?' asked Angie.

'Lots of stuff?' asked Minna.

'She got a pen,' said George. 'Oh, and a **thunder cloud**.' He glanced up at the clear blue sky.

'Anything else?' asked Angie.

Philomena was tempted to say she'd been given a beautiful black horse for her birthday, but she didn't.

'I think a pen is a good present,' said George.

'At least it's better than a thunder cloud,' said Angie.

Sarah (with an 'H') Sullivan, who was standing nearby with her friends, overheard them and turned around.

'Who got a thunder cloud for their birthday?' she said.

21

Sarah Sullivan was definitely *not* one of Philomena's best friends.

'Nobody,' said George. 'But Philomena got a pen.'

'Was that *all* you got?' asked Sarah, who was something of an expert when it came to presents. Her mother owned a gift shop.

'Yes,' said Philomena.

'Was it a *wonder* pen?' joked Sarah.

Some of her classmates laughed, but Philomena was too s h o c k e d to react.

How did Sarah know? Now everyone would laugh at her for getting such an ordinary present.

'I suppose George Creek will get a creek for his birthday,' said Sarah.

Philomena put her arm around George and said, 'I'd buy George the biggest creek in the world.'

'You can't buy creeks, Philomena Daydreamer,' said Sarah.

'And George's creek would have chocolate ice-cream running through it,' continued Philomena. 'Any time he was hungry, he could go down and scoop up an enormous bowl of yummy, delicious . . .'

Philomena never got to finish her sentence. A big, hairy hand landed on her shoulder. She turned around to see the owner of the hand. It was her teacher, Mr Flower. His moustache seemed crooked. His nose looked ꮪꮇꭒꮷꮆꭼꭱ. He had scribbly lines all over his forehead. These were bad signs. Someone had drawn the grumps on Mr Flower this morning.

'Head in the clouds again, Philomena Wonderpen?' said Mr Flower.

Philomena nodded. It was true.

The teacher clapped his hands. 'Class! Inside, please,' he said.

As they filed into the classroom, Sarah Sullivan whispered, 'And Mr Flower would get a flower for his birthday.'

Mr Flower didn't hear her. Mr Flower *never* heard Sarah's jokes. He wrote 'HARD WORK' in big letters on the chalkboard. They all sat down.

'One day you will all grow up to be big like me,' he said.

Sarah Sullivan nodded her head. Some of the fidgety boys at the back pretended to faint. The rest of the class felt a bad mood coming on.

'And if there's one thing big people know,' said Mr Flower, 'it's how to work hard and concentrate.'

George shot his hand into the air. He wanted to point out that Mr Flower

had said *two* things. Philomena tugged on his shirt and whispered, 'Not now, George.'

'Can I tell him it's your birthday, then?' he whispered back.

They both looked over at the empty birthday chair. Philomena shrugged. George was about to shoot his hand into the air again, when Mr Flower thumped the chalkboard.

'Sums!' he said in a voice that rolled like thunder.

Now the fidgety boys fell backwards from the force of his voice. Mr Flower started writing very hard sums on the board. There were groans all around, until he pointed to a large sign over the door that said:

'No Groaning'.

Philomena stared at the very long, very hard sums. They looked like tangled wool to her. All twisted and knotted. She reached for her wonder pen.

'Is that your birthday present?' whispered Angie.

'Can I hold it?' asked Minna.

'Um, maybe later,' said Philomena.

She wasn't sure why, but it didn't seem a good idea

to let anyone else hold her wonder pen. Mr Flower stood watching them from the front of the room. He rocked back and forth. He balanced on his tippy-toes like an acrobat. There was a sign behind him that said:

'No Acrobatics'.

Philomena didn't mention it.

She drew a zero.

That was a good start for sums. Of course, the zero would look much better as a face.

So she drew a few dots.

They became eyes.

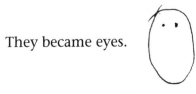

She drew some ears.

Then some hair.

Now the zero looked like Sarah Sullivan.

'She needs a long nose,' thought Philomena. 'So long that she'd have to carry it around in a wheelbarrow.'

Philomena started to draw a long nose . . .

'Philomena!'

It was Mr Flower, interrupting a very funny daydream.

'Yes?' she said, hiding her drawing.

'You are smiling,' said Mr Flower. 'People do not smile when they are doing hard sums.'

George Creek shot his hand in the air. 'Philomena is smiling because today is her birthday,' he said.

Then Angie put her hand up and said, 'She's eight.' Just in case Mr Flower didn't know this.

'Today,' said Minna, to make the point perfectly clear.

'Oh . . .' said Mr Flower. He looked a little embarrassed. 'I'd quite forgotten about that.'

Then he **twitched** his moustache and pointed to the 'No Daydreaming' sign above his desk. 'You can sit in the birthday chair *after* you have stopped daydreaming and finished your sums, Philomena,' he said. 'It is, after all, a very important job. A sensible, responsible job.'

Philomena went red in the face. She'd *never* get to sit in the birthday chair now. If only she was the teacher. Then she'd let herself sit in the birthday chair all day.

And she'd have a sign that said:

'No Rules'.

Philomena picked up her wonder pen. This time she deliberately drew a line instead of sums. Then she drew another and another, until she'd drawn her classroom. Sarah Sullivan leaned over to look at her drawing.

'That's not very good,' she whispered.

'Shhh,' said Philomena. 'I'm concentrating.'

'Why don't you draw something interesting?' said Sarah.

Philomena wrapped her arms around her drawing. Sarah Sullivan (art critic) went back to her work.

'This is more than a drawing,' thought Philomena.

She drew desks and chairs and children. She even drew Mr Flower, only he didn't look the right size. But Philomena wasn't worried about that. There was one more very important thing she had to draw. Her heart started racing. She took a deep breath, then drew *herself* as the teacher. She would be Miss Wonderpen, and she would be the best teacher in the world.

If only it would come true. 'Why are all the nicest things only daydreams?' she wondered. Like being the teacher and having a private ice-cream creek and owning a beautiful horse called Black Thunder. She closed her eyes. If she dreamed as hard as she could, would this dream come true? Philomena worked her brain more than she ever would for sums.

Mr Flower would be pleased with how hard she was concentrating. She dreamed so hard, she didn't notice a hand reach across the table and pick up her wonder pen. She didn't see the hand start drawing on her picture. It added a sleeping secret to the

No Riots

classroom scene, with just the slightest twitch in
its tail.

Philomena opened her eyes. Her brain felt like it
was about to **burst.**

Just then a butterfly landed on her hand and tickled
her. It had beautiful stripy wings. And it *didn't* look like
a moth.

'Hello,' whispered Philomena. 'You were meant to
tickle George Creek, not me.'

The butterfly didn't answer her. Philomena looked
down at her classroom drawing. 'You know, butterfly,'
she said, 'if I could have one birthday wish, then
I wish this daydream would come true.'

chapter 5

A loud burst of laughter broke through the classroom. Philomena looked up to see what was so funny. All the children were staring at her.

'What's wrong?' she asked.

George put his hand up. 'Why are you sitting at a table, Miss?' he said.

'You called me Miss.'

This caused another great burst of laughter. Philomena looked around the room. It seemed smaller. Had all the chairs and desks shrunk? Or . . . ? Could it be . . . ? She looked down at her wonder pen. It was

glowing

a bright, golden colour.

Melissa DiGeorgio put her hand up. 'Miss, Miss,' she said. 'Can we have story time now?'

Philomena stood up and her knees

b^u m pe d

against the table. There was something strange about her legs. They were longer than usual. She reached up her arms. Her hands almost touched the ceiling.

'Where's Mr Flower?' asked Philomena.

The class broke into laughter again.

'You mean Johnny Flower?' said Sarah Sullivan. She pointed to the corner table where only the

wriggliest

children ever sat. There, right at the back, was a boy with a long moustache. He was trying to do hard sums. Philomena started giggling. She couldn't help it. Mr Flower looked so small.

Then she realised that Mr Flower was a student. So, who was the teacher? Was it . . . her? Philomena looked at the drawing of her class with *herself* as the teacher. This was the best daydream in the whole world!

'Okay, everyone,' said Philomena. 'If I'm the teacher, then . . . sit on the floor.'

She thought they'd ignore her, but her classmates came and sat on the floor. Even Sarah Sullivan.

Philomena smiled. She could make them do anything she wanted.

'Stand up,' she said.

The children all stood.

'Sit down.'

They sat.

'Stand up.'

The children got to their feet. Philomena nearly giggled again, until she remembered that teachers do not giggle.

'Sit down.'

They sat, but a few started complaining. 'Aw, Miss . . .'

'It's true,' thought Philomena. 'I *am* the teacher.'

But that meant she'd have to know all about sums

and write sensible things on the chalkboard. Could she do that? Where did she begin? Philomena went to the spot where Mr Flower usually stood. That seemed like a good start. Now what should she do? The class was staring at her,  so she stared back.

They stared harder.

She stared even harder back.

This was fun. She didn't usually win staring contests. Some of the children started **wriggling** on their bottoms, waiting for her to say something.

George was about to offer a helpful suggestion when Sarah Sullivan spoke in a very loud whisper. 'I think Miss is daydreaming again.'

The children laughed. Philomena was cross.
'Oh ha, ha, Sarah Smarty-van!' she said.

Sarah looked as if she'd been knocked over. She went red in the face and tears started welling in her eyes.

'Uh oh,' thought Philomena.

Teachers did not taunt children. And they never called them names.

'You see, class,' said Philomena, thinking quickly, 'calling each other names hurts feelings. That is why we should never do it.'

Sarah blinked a few times. The class blinked a few more times. Everyone thought about this clever thing their teacher had just said. They all started nodding their heads. Then George shot his hand into the air. 'Miss! Miss! Are we going to have that story now?'

Trust George to remind her. Philomena wasn't sure if she was up to reading a proper story. She sometimes stumbled over words, especially big ones.

The class was growing more restless. Boys started hooting at the top of their voices. Girls started calling to friends across the room. Johnny Flower was

meowing loudly like a kitten.

There was even the sound of low, grumbling snoring!

This would turn into a riot any second. And there was a ' **No Riots** '

sign at the back of the room.

A knock at the door made everyone stop their racket to see who was there. It was a woman holding a brown paper bag in her hand.

'Yes?' said Philomena.

'Excuse me,' said the woman. 'My Johnny forgot his lunch today.' Then she went over to Mr Flower, whose face was turning red.

'Aw . . . Mum!' he said. 'How embarrassing.'

Mrs Flower dropped the brown paper bag into her son's lap, then said, 'Do try to behave today, Johnny.' She gave him a huge kiss on his moustache.

The class went

'Whoo!'

And another kiss.

The class went 'Aaah!'

38

Mrs Flower left the room. The children started hooting and laughing again. It was hurting Philomena's ears. She put her fingers in her mouth and whistled the way her mum had taught her. The hooters swallowed their hoots, the gigglers sat with their mouths open, but the snorer still snored quietly in a corner.

'I have something important to tell you,' said Philomena.

She told them it was a 'Have Fun' and 'No Rules' day. The class broke into a big cheer. They bounced and bopped, and were certain to start their hooting again when Minna Lim suddenly jerked her head forward and yelled, 'Stop it!'

Little Johnny Flower was pulling on Minna's beautiful pigtails, making a 'Whoo-hoo' train noise. Now Philomena was mad again. Nobody was mean to her friends.

'You!' said Philomena, pointing to her teacher. 'Go to the corner chair and write your name in the red book.'

There was a loud gasp from all the children.

Not the **RED BOOK**.

Only children caught doing something *extremely* bad were made

to write their names in the red book. Johnny Flower
looked up at Philomena with sad eyes. Then he
shuffled to his doom.

'Oh dear,' thought Philomena. 'I've used a rule.'
This was not the sort of birthday she wanted to have.
She didn't know if she liked being the big person. She
wanted to sit down with her friends and put her arm
around Minna's shoulder.

Did big people ever feel as confused as she felt now?
Maybe she could run home. Philomena turned towards
the door, but there was no escape. A pair of sensible
shoes had just stepped into the classroom.

The Principal was at the doorway.

Mrs Bustier.

chapter 6

Mrs Bustier was a large woman with a stern face and an even sterner hairdo. She wore glasses that looked annoyed with the world. And she had an expression to match. Her shoes were **tight** and her mouth never smiled. Nobody did anything to make Mrs Bustier mad.

'Miss Wonderpen,' said Mrs Bustier.

Philomena gulped. Uh oh. She was in BIG trouble now. Pretending to be the teacher. Making children write their names in the red book. Dreaming up a 'No Rules' day when everyone knows that schools have rules. Lots and lots of them. What would Mrs Bustier do? Take her to the office? Make up a whole new red book for students who thought they were teachers?

The Principal waved her hand. 'A word, please,' she said.

Philomena walked over, her legs **shaking** with each step.

'There have been reports of butterflies in other classrooms,' said Mrs Bustier.

'Yes,' squeaked Philomena.

'Do make sure that you capture a few if you see any,' said Mrs Bustier. 'They will make good specimens for you to study with your class.'

Your class?

Mrs Bustier wasn't angry after all. And she thought that Philomena was a teacher, too. This really *was* the best daydream in the world.

Just then the snoring sound in the corner grew louder. Philomena frowned. Wait a minute. She didn't order any snoring in her daydream. Something wasn't right.

Suddenly the snore broke into a tremendous snort, which ended in a long, low grumble.

'What in the name of blazes was that?' asked Mrs Bustier.

Philomena shook her head. 'I don't know.'

Mrs Bustier didn't seem at all pleased with that answer. She glared at the classroom. 'Who is snoring?' she asked.

No one spoke.

'Do you want me to put up a 'No Snoring' sign?' asked Philomena.

'I'll spell it,' said Sarah Sullivan.

'There's always room for one more rule,' said Mrs Bustier.

Then she spotted Johnny Flower with the **RED BOOK**. He'd written his name and crime (pulling pigtails) on an empty page. Mrs Bustier forgot about the new rule and looked at him through narrow eyes.

'Is that Flower boy causing you trouble?' she whispered.

'Not really,' said Philomena. She felt sorry for him now.

Mrs Bustier *leaned* a little closer. Philomena caught a whiff of her perfume. It smelt bothered.

'He's a dreamer and a fidget,' whispered Mrs Bustier. 'Always will be. A leopard can't change its spots.'

Then the Principal winked. Philomena blushed. She'd never been winked at by a Principal before. Mrs Bustier turned to the class and started a long lecture about snoring and staying awake. Philomena tried to concentrate. She was, after all, the teacher. But she heard a strange noise outside. It sounded like a horse. A big horse.

Everyone ran to the window.

'This school is turning into a circus,' said Mrs Bustier.

Philomena looked over the heads of her classmates and caught sight of a beautiful black horse vanishing round the corner. It was being chased by a man who looked a lot like her dad.

'Black Thunder,' she whispered. What was he doing in her daydream? Unless this wasn't a daydream at all . . .

She picked up her wonder pen. The swirling, coloured lines were more beautiful than ever. A picture started forming in her head. She'd drawn herself as the teacher with this pen. Now everyone thought she *was* the teacher.

And this morning she'd drawn a horse called Black Thunder. Now her dad was chasing a horse down the road.

And the butterflies. In the car she'd drawn lots of butterflies. Now Mrs Bustier was asking her to catch them for experiments. Philomena looked down at her wonder pen, and the picture became bright and clear. This was no ordinary pen – it was a *magical* pen that made drawings come to life!

'That's what Dad was trying to tell me,' she muttered.

Mrs Bustier clapped her hands loudly, and everyone jumped. **'Sit down at once!'** barked the Principal.

Her voice was so loud and scary that all the students scrambled back to their seats. Even Philomena tried to sit at her seat, until she remembered that she was the teacher. Then Mrs Bustier gave Johnny Flower one last stern look and left the room. Everyone breathed a sigh of relief. The snorer snored happily.

Philomena looked at all the rules on the walls. She looked at her classmates. They seemed so small under the signs. So she said the one thing she'd always wanted a teacher to say.

'Let's not do any work today.'

The class cheered. Philomena felt her whole face light up with a smile. This was more like it. This was what a birthday was all about. She forgot about the Principal. She forgot about the rules.

'In fact,' she said, 'let's go outside to play. Now!'

They didn't need to be told twice. All the children scattered and clambered outside. Philomena grabbed some paper, just in case she wanted to draw that chocolate creek. Then she followed them. In the corner of the classroom a snoring creature grumbled once and started to wake up.

chapter 7

No one saw the snorer wake. They were too busy on the play equipment. Children were climbing over the wooden fort. Some were hanging upside down from the bars. Some slid down the slippery dip headfirst.

Philomena thought this was the most perfect school day she could ever imagine. George, Angie and Minna were sitting on top of the long ladder that stretched from the fort to the new climbing frame. They were laughing at a joke.

Philomena rushed over to her friends, but when they saw her coming they went very quiet.

'What were you laughing at?' said Philomena, a big grin on her face.

'Nothing, Miss,' said George.

'We didn't do anything wrong,' said Minna.

'We were just having fun,' said Angie.

'I know, I know,' said Philomena. 'I want to have some fun, too.'

They looked at her as if
she'd said the strangest thing.
Then Minna started giggling behind her
hand. George joined in.

'What?' said Philomena.

'No offence, Miss,' said Angie, 'but you could go to
the staff room and have fun with Mrs Bustier.'

Philomena stared at Angie. How could she say that?
They were best friends. But then she realised, teachers
and students were never *best* friends. She sighed and
walked away. Maybe being the teacher wasn't going to
be as much fun as she thought.

Philomena watched her classmates r**u**n**n**i**ng**

and **climbing** and

leaping.

Johnny Flower had made his way to the top of the fort and was standing on either side of the pointy roof. It looked a bit scary. Then he stood with one foot on the very point of the roof and started balancing like an acrobat. He was rather good at it. Philomena wanted to cheer, but Sarah Sullivan called out, 'Miss! Shouldn't you say something to him?'

Philomena nodded her head. Of course. That would be the sensible thing to do. But what should she say? 'Get down at once!' And then what? Another rule? 'No Balancing on Pointy Roofs'? She remembered what Mrs Bustier had said about leopards not changing their spots. Philomena looked at Mr Flower's magnificent trick. His spots were quite wonderful, really.

Angie and Minna started climbing up to join Mr Flower. They slithered and scrambled on the slippery roof, laughing themselves silly.

Philomena's heart missed a beat or two. Perhaps it *was* time for a wise thing to be said. But she'd had so little practice. Sarah Sullivan should have been the teacher. She always followed the rules. And she *never* had her head in the clouds.

Johnny Flower was waving his arms now,

shouting, 'Look at me, Miss!'

Then a dreadful thing happened. His foot came off the pointy bit. He started slipping, then sliding, then slipping and sliding. He fell onto his bottom and slithered down the roof.

And who was right below him in his flight path?

Angie and Minna.

'Oh no!' yelled Philomena.

Johnny Flower crashed into her two friends, and they all slid to the very edge of the roof, where they teetered and wobbled. It was a long way to the ground.

'Oh dear, oh dear,' said Philomena.

This was terrible. This was a disaster. And it was all her fault. She wasn't a fun teacher, she was a terrible teacher. Could things possibly get worse?

Just then Philomena heard an awful, chilling

She turned to see what was making such a loud, scary noise. The snorer was awake.

He was a lion.

And he looked

HUNGRY!

chapter 8

All the children screamed at once. Even Philomena
screamed. Everyone ran for the trees, for the fort, for
the climbing frame – anything to get away from the
lion. He was walking slowly through the play area.
His tail twitched from side to side. His whiskers
vibrated. His stomach rumbled. It sounded empty.

Some of the smaller children were trying to reach
the lower branches of a tree.

They **jumped** and **jumped** but couldn't make it.
Philomena ran over and lifted them up
one by one.

'Thanks, Miss,' said My Tran. 'You're so tall.'

When the last of the smaller children was safely placed in the tree, Philomena breathed a sigh of relief. Maybe she wasn't such a bad teacher after all. Then she felt something flick against her leg. It was the lion's tail!

'**Yikes!**' she yelled. She scrambled her way to the long ladder that stretched its way across to the fort. Sarah Sullivan was on the ladder, too. She turned to Philomena and said, 'You have to make the lion go away now, Miss.'

'*Me*?' said Philomena. She didn't know how to make a hungry lion go away. 'What are lions scared of?' she asked.

'Scary faces?' said Suzy Miller.

'Kissy-kissy love songs?' called out George.

Philomena thought they were both worth a try. She climbed down a little way, pulled her mouth out wide and sang a sappy song.

The lion didn't seem scared at all. In fact, he grumbled deep and low, then placed his front paws on the lower rung of the climbing frame.

'Help!' cried the children.

'It's climbing!' cried Sarah.

Philomena wanted to run to the highest point of the fort and hide until a teacher came to rescue them. But *she* was the teacher. All the children were looking at her. There must be a way to get rid of the lion.

Then she remembered her wonder pen. It was magic. All she had to do was draw the lion *out* of the playground. She took out the sheets of paper and began to draw.

Her hands were **shaking.**

Her knees **wobbled.** The fort came out looking more like a rocket ship. The ladder looked like a pencil. It was a terrible drawing. Philomena finished and waited for the magic. But . . .

Nothing happened.

'What am I doing wrong?' she cried. The magic had worked for Black Thunder and the butterflies. 'Why isn't it working now?'

She pulled out another sheet of paper, and the drawing of Sarah Sullivan with the long nose slipped out. Philomena picked it up. She'd drawn that with the wonder pen, too, but it hadn't come true. 'Maybe I need more than just a drawing,' she thought. But what?

Before she could answer that question, there was a terrible cry of 'Help!'

It was Angie. She was still clinging to the fort roof with Minna and Johnny Flower. Philomena had quite forgotten about them. The lion had given up climbing the ladder and was now prowling hungrily beneath the three dangling children. They couldn't hold on for much longer.

There was no time to figure out how to make the wonder pen work. Philomena had to make the lion go away. There must be something it was scared of. A big creature, perhaps? A big, black creature . . . Philomena gasped. She realised there *was* such a creature. He was running around in the streets.

'Black Thunder!' she cried.

Sarah Sullivan rolled her eyes. 'Still got your head in the clouds, Miss,' she said.

'I'll show you,' said Philomena. 'Sometimes clouds are exactly what we need!' She stood up on the ladder and yelled again in her biggest voice, 'Black Thunder!'

There was a loud whinny from the street. A beautiful black horse with white socks and a white diamond on his nose ran into the playground. He galloped around the play equipment at full speed, then came to a dramatic halt under the fort roof. Dust flew everywhere. Angie, Minna and Johnny Flower finally let go.

Plop! Plop! Plop!

They fell onto Black Thunder's back.

The children cheered. The lion took one look at the huge black horse and decided to go sniff the sandpit.

'Oh, Black Thunder,' sighed Philomena. 'You're the best drawing I've ever done!'

Maybe the day could even go back to being fun now? All the children were safe. And Black Thunder was there. What else could go wrong?

A loud voice bellowed across the playground. It was scarier than a growling lion. It made Philomena's heart miss a beat. It even made Black Thunder shudder.

'MISS WONDERPEN!'

It was Mrs Bustier.

chapter 9

The Principal strode across the playground. Her hairdo wobbled. It looked infuriated. 'Come here, Miss Wonderpen!' called Mrs Bustier.

'I can't,' said Philomena. 'There's a lion!' She pointed to the king of the playground.

'A lion?' roared the Principal.

The lion lay down in the sandpit with his paws over his ears.

Black Thunder shook his head. He'd never heard such a loud noise. The children on the ladder wanted to get away from the Principal. George Creek slipped down onto the back of the beautiful stallion. The others joined him.

'What are those children doing on a horse?' cried Mrs Bustier.

Black Thunder started galloping around the playground.

'Circus tricks!' shouted Johnny Flower.

His words were like electricity. The children formed
a pyramid on Black Thunder's back. Johnny Flower
was the best balancer of them all. Philomena clapped
her hands.

'Miss Wonderpen!' cried Mrs Bustier.
'You are the *naughtiest* teacher I've
ever seen. You have children
doing acrobatics on
a horse. You have

children climbing the fort roof. *And* you have a lion in the schoolyard without permission.'

'I can explain . . .' started Philomena.

'That will not be necessary,' said Mrs Bustier. She clapped her hands. A gang of teachers came out from the tearoom where they'd been hiding from the lion.

'Advance!' cried Mrs Bustier.

'Do we have to?' said the teachers.

'NOW!'

The gang started moving forward. Some made their way towards Philomena. Some headed for Black Thunder with a long rope. They stretched the rope out across the playground. Philomena shouted for Black Thunder to 'Watch out!' but the mighty stallion leapt over it gracefully.

She knew the teachers would never catch Black Thunder. But what about the ones who were coming to capture her? Then she heard

a tremendous

roar.

Uh oh. The teachers had run into the lion. He had them cornered in the sandpit.

'Yikes,' said Philomena. 'Now what?'

'Dream up another crazy idea,' muttered Sarah Sullivan.

Philomena glared at her. Sarah was eating a salami and watercress sandwich. (Her mother was very creative with lunch.) Trust Sarah to be sensible and bring a snack.

'You want a crazy idea?' said Philomena.

Sarah shrugged.

Philomena leapt across the ladder before Sarah could take another bite. She grabbed the sandwich and jumped onto the ground.

The king of the playground stopped growling at the teachers and turned to face her.

'Oops,' said Philomena. 'Maybe this was too crazy.' All she had to protect herself was a salami and watercress sandwich.

'Want this?' she said, holding out Sarah's lunch.

The lion nodded his head. Philomena threw the sandwich into the fort.

The king of the beasts **growled**,

then leapt into the fort and started gobbling. Philomena shut the fort gate.

'Well done, Miss,' cried George Creek as Black Thunder galloped past.

Philomena wiped her brow. It was time to make everything go back to normal. She took out her wonder pen and headed for the ladder. But a hand reached out and **SNatchEd** the pen away. Then another hand grabbed her by the arm. It was the gang of teachers.

'No, you don't understand,' said Philomena. 'I have to draw us out of trouble.'

'You're coming with us,' said the biggest teacher.

Philomena pleaded, but the teachers wouldn't listen.

Not even
being a grown-
up was going to get her
out of this mess.

'I'll help you, Miss,'

came a mighty cry. It was Johnny Flower. He leapt
from Black Thunder's back, did a triple somersault in
the air, and landed in front of the teachers. They were
so amazed, they let go of Philomena. Johnny saw his

chance and grabbed the wonder pen. He handed it back to her.

'Thank you,' she said. 'You know, you're really very good at acrobatics.'

Johnny Flower blushed. 'That's what I want to be when I grow up, Miss,' he said. He did some more backflips and forward rolls. The teachers stood and stared.

Philomena quickly climbed back up the ladder.

Now she'd have to draw faster than ever before. Out of the corner of her eye she could see the Principal heading straight for her. She made her wonder pen fly across the page.

'Why are you drawing?' said Sarah Sullivan.

'To save us,' said Philomena. 'You should really try drawing sometime. You stare at a blank piece of paper and let your mind start *dreaming*.'

'Leave Miss alone! She's a good drawer,' called out George, whizzing by on Black Thunder again. **'And that's a faaaact!'**

Philomena knew she had to do more than just a good drawing this time. She had to make everything right. Make it better. Wasn't that why she had a magic pen in the first place?

She let her mind go crazy with unusual and wonderful ideas. She drew so fast, her hand was like a

'Watch out!' cried Minna.

Oh no! Mrs Bustier had rounded up the gang of teachers. They were heading across the ladder with a soccer net in their hands. Philomena looked at her drawing. There was still plenty to do.

'I need time,' she said. 'More time.'

Black Thunder neighed. He raced under the teachers, kicking up a tremendous cloud of dust. The dust flew into the teachers' eyes. They teetered on the ladder.

Philomena drew faster.

Lines **raced** across the page.

Swirls and squiggles appeared like lightning.

But the gang of teachers tied handkerchiefs around their faces. Black Thunder's dust didn't bother them now. The mighty stallion neighed towards Philomena as if to say, 'Sorry!' She was on her own.

Philomena drew like a hurricane. There were children on the paper, and teachers, and the fort, and a little ginger surprise . . .

'Stop this nonsense at ONCE!'

Mrs Bustier was standing over her. Philomena put her pen down and stared at her picture. She wanted to cry. The drawing was finished. She just didn't know how to bring it to life.

'You are coming with me,' said Mrs Bustier.

'It's not fair!' cried Philomena. 'My dad would know how to make this drawing come to life. Great Grandfather Rufus would know. I'm not even good at being a Wonderpen.'

Philomena hung her head. Now she'd be given teacher detention. And she'd never get to be a child again. 'If only I'd been more sensible,' she moaned, 'instead of always wishing for things that really should *not* be there.'

'We do not *wish* in this school, Miss Wonderpen,' said Mrs Bustier.

Suddenly Philomena looked up excitedly. Mrs Bustier had just given her the answer – the last magic thing that would make the wonder pen work. She stood up and held her drawing high in the air. Then she shouted,

'I wish!'

Philomena opened her eyes. When she looked around the playground, she almost fell from the ladder with laughter. The most beautiful sight greeted her.

Her classmates were making human pyramids on a gym mat. Mr Flower watched them, a proud look on his face. He was **BIG**. He was the teacher again.

'Four plus three plus two plus one,' he said. 'That's a human pyramid sum.'

He looked up at Philomena, a pink blush to his cheeks. 'Head in the clouds again, Miss Wonderpen?' he asked.

Philomena looked down at herself. Oops! She was still big. In her rush to finish the drawing, she'd forgotten to make herself little again. Mr Flower must think she was still a teacher.

Philomena jumped down from the ladder. Next to the playground was an ice-cream van with a large sign that read:

FREE ICE-CREM

'Double oops!' thought Philomena. She must have made a spelling mistake.

She walked over to the ice-cream van. A large woman was behind the counter. She had a very friendly hairdo.

'What flavour would you like, Miss Wonderpen?' asked Mrs Bustier.

'Blueberry, please.'

Mrs Bustier handed Philomena a free blueberry ice-cream. It was delicious, although a little bit firm.

Philomena walked past the fort where she heard a tiny meow. A beautiful ginger kitten was pawing

at a salami sandwich. It had a little furry mane around its neck.

'Nice Kitty,' said Philomena. 'No more **roaring** for you.'

The kitten purred as Philomena wandered over to where some teachers were offering rides on Black Thunder's back.

'I think it's my turn now,' she said.

She climbed onto the back of her mighty stallion, leaned over and whispered in his ear, 'Now run like the wind, boy.' And he did.

***

Philomena found Dad in the street halfway home. He didn't have to ask why she looked like a grown-up. He understood straightaway. After all, he *was* a Wonderpen, and he'd been given his own pen on his eighth birthday, just like Philomena.

'Done a good drawing lately?' he asked.

Philomena told Dad all about being the teacher, about the lion that somebody else drew, and about the free ice-cream. Dad laughed.

'Your Great Grandfather Rufus went to the moon on his eighth birthday,' he said.

'Really?' said Philomena. 'Why didn't I think of that?'

'Easy does it,' said Dad, smiling.

He **climbed** onto Black Thunder's

back to join Philomena. 'I think we'd better go back to your school and get you back to size,'
he said.

'Yes, please,' said Philomena. 'Being big is not as much fun as I thought it would be.'

As they trotted down the road, Dad told her about some of the mischief he got up to with his wonder pen. 'I'm afraid I turned your grandmother into a dog on my eighth birthday.'

Philomena laughed. She thought about her wonderful family and their pens. 'Dad,' she said, 'the wonder pens you make in the factory. They're not . . .'

'Magic?' he said. 'No. Afraid not. Just copies.'

Philomena wondered if she could draw a picture that gave every child in the world a *magic* wonder pen. It was an amazing thought. Then she looked up and saw they'd arrived at school.

'How do I make everything normal again?' she asked.

'Just fold the drawing over,' said Dad. 'The magic stops.'

Philomena found all her drawings and placed them on her lap. First she folded her butterflies drawing. Then she folded the playground picture.

In an instant the playground went back to normal. No more ICE-CREM van. No more pyramids. No more fun. Mrs Bustier became her stern self again.

But there was a low, *rumbling* lion-growl from inside the fort.

'Oops,' said Philomena. 'The kitten's turned into a lion again.' She quickly found the classroom picture and folded it over. When she looked up the fort was empty – the lion had gone back to being a drawing. Then Philomena noticed the size of her arms and legs. She was back to being a child.

Mr Flower stood in the middle of the playground with a confused expression on his face. 'How did we get out here?' he muttered. Then he clapped his hands. 'Time to go back to class,' he said. 'We have sums to do!'

Philomena sighed. 'I was never a bossy teacher,' she said.

George laughed beside her. 'Teacher? You? Are you daydreaming again, Philomena?' he asked.

Philomena looked at Dad. He winked at her and whispered, 'They won't remember what happened. That's the way it works.'

'It's too bad the magic has to stop completely,' Philomena whispered back.

Suddenly Mr Flower stopped clapping his hands and

barking orders. He had a strange smile on his face. 'I think that tomorrow,' he said, 'we will learn how to make human pyramids for maths.' Then he mumbled, 'I could have been an acrobat myself . . .'

Dad gave Philomena a hug goodbye. 'Maybe a little of the magic rubbed off, after all,' he said.

chapter 11

The rest of Philomena's birthday was almost perfect.
Mr Flower seemed to have a smile painted on his face
all afternoon. He even took down the

'No Acrobatics'

sign and asked Sarah Sullivan to draw a picture
on the back.

Philomena got to sit in the birthday
chair. She let George tell *three*
facts in the class meeting.
After school Mrs Creek
treated Philomena and
George to chocolate
ice-creams.

Now Philomena was
sitting on the couch
with Mum and Dad.
Tobias was asleep
between them.

They'd just had yummy pizza for dinner.

Philomena wore a big grin.

'This has been the best day ever!' she said.

Dad wrapped his arm around her. 'I'm glad, sweetheart. Having a wonder pen is a special thing,' he said. 'But . . .'

'I know, I know,' said Philomena. 'No more lions.'

'And no more Miss Wonderpen, either,' said Mum.

'That's okay,' said Philomena. 'There's heaps of other pictures in my head. I can draw sunny days for the rest of the year. Or a new car for everyone in the street. Or even better! I can draw lots and lots of food for the WHOLE WORLD and no one will be hungry or anything...'

Philomena interrupted her own daydream to look for her pen. She couldn't wait to get started.

Dad sighed. 'Those would be very big drawings, darling,' he said. 'Too big for you and me.'

'Oh,' said Philomena.

Maybe Dad was right. It was too hard to draw the whole world. Where would she find enough paper? But she could still do lots of small pictures. She closed her eyes and wondered how to draw a moon-cloud. One that would *tickle* anyone who was feeling a bit low. It was a lovely dream, and she was just drifting off when Dad nudged her and said it was time for sleep.

Philomena kissed her parents goodnight and crawled into bed. Under the pillow was the drawing of Black Thunder. It had been the hardest of her pictures to fold, until Mum told her a Wonderpen secret. Any time she wanted to see her mighty friend again, all she had to do was unfold the drawing and say the magic words. It was late, and she really was very tired, but she was eight now. And that meant she had just a little more energy than yesterday.

She sat up and took out her drawing.

'I wish,' she whispered.

As she trotted down the driveway on Black Thunder's back, she saw Dad leaning on their fence. 'Going for a ride?' he said.

'Can I please, Dad?'

'Just up and down the street.'

Philomena leaned against Black Thunder's neck. She didn't see a sneaky hand back in her room open her special drawer and remove the wonder pen from its box.

'Run like the wind, boy,' she said.

The trees flashed by, and the wind blew in her face. Philomena knew that Black Thunder would always be the most beautiful drawing she'd ever made come true.

And the sneaky hand? Well, that's another drawing . . .

From Ian Bone

I was always daydreaming as a boy and would often be told to 'stop looking out the window' by my teachers. Like Philomena, I looove daydreaming.

Philomena Wonderpen came to me as an idea one day. The idea set up a campsite in my brain and started cooking up other juicy ideas to go with it. If there's one thing I love more than daydreams, it's the smell of juicy ideas. So, I just HAD to write Philomena's story.

From Janine Dawson

While Ian was 'looking out the window', chances are I was the kid who'd already been sent out of the class for daydreaming! My teachers used to tell me to stop daydreaming all the time. Luckily, I mustn't have been listening, because I still daydream and draw all the time, only now they call that 'being an illustrator'!

Watch out for the next fantastic Philomena adventure:

Philomena wonderpen is a teeny weeny doll